The Doctor

By Jenny Giles
Photographs by Lindsay Edwards

I am going to the doctor.
My ear is hurting.

Dad is coming with me.

Medical
Clinic
Specialist Family Ph
Switc
Book an appointment online
anytime, anywhere!
• No waiting for the clinic to open
• No waiting on hold
Download our App
iTunes
Eastbound Medical

I sit with Dad

in the waiting room.

We read some books,

and we wait to see the doctor.

I go into the doctor’s room
with Dad.
We sit down,
and Dad talks to the doctor.
I can see a **stethoscope**.

My ear is hurting again.

The doctor talks to me.

I climb up onto the bed.
The doctor looks into my ear
with her little light.

She can see that my ear
is very red inside.

The doctor looks

into my mouth, too.

I stay very still

for the doctor.

She puts her stethoscope
on my back.
The stethoscope
is cold!

Then, I sit down on the chair

by Dad,

and the doctor

talks to us again.

My ear is still hurting,
but the doctor says
that some **medicine**
will make it better.

I will have to take the medicine
for seven days.
Then my ear will be better.

Glossary

medicine

stethoscope

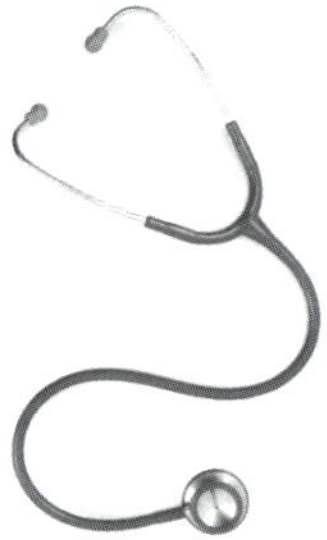